Simon & Schuster
Aunt Izzy – Reprint
Dir 48 – 48696-1
Baskervile + infants
gmb

Text copyright © 1990 Denny Robson
Illustrations copyright © 1990 Jan Lewis

First published in Great Britain in 1990
by Simon & Schuster Young Books
Reprinted 1991, 1992 and 1994

Photoset in 18pt Baskerville by
Goodfellow & Egan Ltd., Cambridge

Printed and bound in Belgium
by Proost International Production

Simon & Schuster Young Books
Campus 400
Maylands Avenue
Hemel Hempstead HP2 7EZ

BRITISH LIBRARY CATALOGUING IN PUBLICATION DATA
Robson, Denny
The Great Aunt Izzy disaster.
I. Title   II. Lewis, Jan
823'.914[J]

ISBN 0-7500-0259-X
ISBN 0-7500-0260-3 Pbk

Denny Robson

THE GREAT AUNT IZZY DISASTER

Illustrated by Jan Lewis

Chapter One

Emmeline Mary McGinty was a
bucketful of trouble. At least her Great
Aunt Izzy said so. The same Great Aunt
Izzy was a stuffy old sock. At least
Emmeline Mary said so.

Emmeline Mary McGinty
liked cheeseburgers,
pop songs, cartoons
and knock knock jokes.

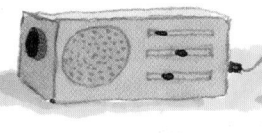

Great Aunt Izzy made
cucumber sandwiches
for tea, liked hymns
in the evenings,
and thought that
children should be very
quiet indeed.

So it wasn't really surprising that
Emmy and Great Aunt Izzy didn't get
on very well. And perhaps it wasn't so
surprising that something rather
strange happened the time Great Aunt
Izzy came to stay.

6

"But why," moaned Emmy for the sixtieth time to Sam, her next door neighbour, "has *Aunt Izzy* been sent to look after me while Mum and Dad are away?"

Sam ignored her and continued waving a shiny pendant in front of Emmy's eyes. His dad had been hypnotised into giving up smoking and he was wondering whether he could hypnotise Emmy into giving up Aunt Izzy moans.

"She doesn't seem to like me much," Emmy went on, "and I think she's very odd."

It was true Aunt Izzy wasn't like anyone else. She was a tall thin old lady, with lines on her forehead you could play noughts and crosses on, and huge big feet that she forced into tiny shoes to make them look dainty. (Emmy thought this was what made her grumpy – she was always much nicer with her slippers on.)

"You are feeling sleepy," said Sam, looking hopeful. Emmy was really going to be a pain this week unless he could make this hypnotising trick work.

Emmy went silent. Sam sat up expectantly.

"No I'm not," said Emmy suddenly, grabbing the pendant. "We're going to have to do something."

"We?" Sam sounded a bit worried. Emmy had got him into lots of trouble before with her funny ideas.

"If we don't, I'll go nuts," Emmy threatened. "I'll start to look like a cucumber sandwich, I'll stop telling you jokes. . . ."

"All right, all right," laughed Sam. "But what can we do?"

They were silent for a few minutes. And then they both looked at the pendant in Emmy's hand.

"We can't," whispered Sam.

"Yes we can," said Emmy. "You can hypnotise her, and when she's in a trance, I'll persuade her that she likes all the things that I like, and then we'll change her back before Mum and Dad get back!"

And that was how the Great Aunt Izzy disaster started. Sam knew there was no point in arguing with Emmy. She never listened. He was to come back after lunch and they would start work on Great Aunt Izzy then.

Chapter Two

"Back again, young man?" exclaimed Great Aunt Izzy, when Sam returned after lunch. "So soon? When I was a girl. . . ."

Aunt Izzy was very fond of "when I was a girl" stories (which were always about how hard and nasty life used to be).

Emmy was still struggling through her cucumber sandwiches.

"Now eat up the
crusts, Emmeline,"
Aunt Izzy boomed,
"or you'll never get
hair like mine."
Emmy looked at Aunt
Izzy's corkscrew frizz
and quietly stuffed
the crusts into a pot plant.

"Before I ate crusts my hair
was completely—"

"Aunt Izzy," Emmy interrupted.
"Sam and I are doing an experiment.
We want to see if we can make you relax
using this pendant." Aunt Izzy looked
suspicious.

"Er, it might make your feet hurt less," Emmy went on. Aunt Izzy, whose feet at that moment were squeezed into a minute pair of pink pumps, looked tempted.

"Well," she said sitting back in her chair. "It can't hurt, I suppose. . . ."

Sam began straight away, before she had time to change her mind.

"*You are feeling sleepy, Aunt Izzy,*" he said in a sing-song voice. Emmy giggled.

"Very sleepy. . . ." he droned, beginning to feel a bit silly. And he was starting to feel very uncomfortable indeed, when suddenly, to his astonishment, Aunt Izzy's chin dropped and she fell asleep!

"We've done it, Emm!" Sam whispered, staring at Aunt Izzy in amazement. "She's in a trance!"

But Emmy didn't reply.

Emmy was fast asleep as well.

"Wake up, Emmy," Sam hissed, as he shook her shoulders. But Emmy didn't move. "The book," he said to himself. "That's it."

He frantically flicked through the pages and read:

"To wake the patient, merely tell them who they are, and that they will awake when you click your fingers."

"Right," he said, turning to Aunt Izzy by mistake in his panic. "You're Emmeline Mary McGinty and you will wake up when I click my fingers!"

He clicked his fingers, and then looked up – to see Great Aunt Izzy waking up!

"Hiya Sam," yawned Aunt Izzy. "I must have dropped off. Is the old dragon in a trance yet?"

Sam froze with horror.

"Emmy McGinty," he said quickly to Emmy. "Wake up now. *Please!*"

Emmy opened her eyes and looked at Sam's panic-stricken face.

"She thinks she's you, Emmy," he said. "I've accidently hypnotised Aunt Izzy into thinking she's you!"

Chapter Three

It couldn't be true, thought Emmy,
staring at Aunt Izzy. But Aunt Izzy
certainly wasn't sitting up as straight as
she usually did. She was sprawling all
over her chair – rather like Emmy
usually did, in fact. And she was
whistling along to a pop song on the
radio!

How could it have happened? Emmy needed to talk to Sam – alone.

"Um, Emmeline Mary," said Emmy, in what she hoped sounded like Aunt Izzy's voice. "I think you should leave the table."

"Might as well," Aunt Izzy giggled. "Can't take it with me."

Amazing, thought Emmy, she even sounds like me.

"Er, go into the other room, Emmeline," Emmy went on, "and see what's on the telly."

"I already know," said Aunt Izzy nudging Sam. "A goldfish bowl and a vase of flowers."

Emmy's eyes opened wider. That was just the sort of thing that she would have said! Aunt Izzy winked at Sam and went into the living room.

"What are we going to do?" groaned Sam. "This is disastrous."

Emmy was looking thoughtful.

"Don't worry," she said finally, with that look in her eye Sam knew always meant trouble. "We can change her back. But not yet. Not until tea-time. Until then, I'm going to be Aunt Izzy and she can be me!"

Chapter Four

Sam shook his head. No way. It was a dreadful idea! He opened his mouth to protest, but Emmy had already disappeared. He found her in the living room, a look of gleeful fascination on her face, watching Aunt Izzy prise off her shoes and put on her own old trainers.

"Amazing," Emmy whispered. "She even ties them like I do."

"We have to stop this, Emmy," Sam hissed from behind her shoulder.

"Incredible," she giggled, as Aunt Izzy's old bones began jumping around to the radio. "She even dances like I do!"

"And if we don't stop this, Emmy McGinty. . . ." Emmy turned round. She knew better than to ignore that tone in Sam's voice.

Sam could be very determined when he wanted to be.

She smiled sweetly. "Just got to go upstairs, Sam."

There was no time to lose. Emmy dashed upstairs and into Aunt Izzy's room. A long black dress hung on the door. She quickly put it on, hitched it up using her school tie as a belt, stuck one foot into a tiny purple satin shoe, yanked it off, decided to stick to trainers, tried to frizz her hair, gave up, pulled an old black hat over her plaits, and then she looked in the mirror. Perfect.

Now for the great outdoors, she thought, sliding silently down the bannisters. She tip-toed past the living room (where Aunt Izzy could be heard loudly singing along to the radio) and out of the front door, before Sam could stop her. She was going to enjoy being an old lady.

Outside, the first thing Emmy did was hobble up to a policeman and ask him if he could see her across the road. The policeman, who immediately recognised Emmy, told her he could see her a mile away looking like that, and walked away laughing.

Then Emmy decided to try out her disguise at the bus stop. A little old lady began to talk to her.

"How long do you think the bus will be?" asked the old lady, looking at her watch.

"About 25 metres I should think," said Emmy, with an innocent look.

The old lady frowned and tapped her hearing aid. She tried again.

"Windy, isn't it?"

"No, it's Thursday," said Emmy with
a giggle, and headed off towards the
corner shop with a mixture of skips and
hobbles.

Mr Grim, the shopkeeper, was a
miserable man who didn't like kids in
his store. He never let Emmy choose
fruit for herself and always gave her the
most bruised apples. Well, he wouldn't
dare be rude to her now, Emmy
thought gleefully.

Emmy began to examine the apples, turning each one over carefully, while out of the corner of her eye she watched Mr Grim twitch impatiently.

But after she'd rearranged two boxes of Granny Smiths, Mr Grim was beginning to peer suspiciously under her hat. Emmy decided it was time to leave.

She started to hobble away, and then, when she was sure he was watching, she leap-frogged over a pile of banana boxes! Mr Grim was so surprised he sat back on his best tomatoes.

Chapter Five

Emmy smiled to herself.
That had been fun.
But on the way back,
she began to feel a
bit uneasy. Maybe she
shouldn't have left
Sam with Aunt Izzy
like that. . . .

And when she got home, she began to
feel distinctly worried. There was no
trace of Sam, or of Great Aunt Izzy.
Where on earth could they be? She
hung the long dress back on Aunt Izzy's
door, and then she dashed up the road
again.

It didn't take long to find them. In fact, it would have been impossible to miss Great Aunt Izzy. There she was, in the playground, surrounded by a huge crowd of kids, hanging like a bat from the climbing frame, and whooping loudly for Sam to join her.

Emmy giggled and looked over to where Sam was sitting on the bench. Sam was whistling. Emmy knew what that meant. Sam always whistled when he sulked.

She sat down next to him. "Sorry I ran off, Sam. It was just too good to miss. . . ."

Sam whistled harder. He'd had a horrid afternoon. First of all, Aunt Izzy had made him dance to a pile of Emmy's records. And then she'd almost dragged him out of the house to the playground. And if that wasn't bad enough, every time he tried to look as if he wasn't with her, she whooped his name loudly. He whistled even harder.

Emmy put her arm through his, and pulled a range of his favourite faces. A smile began to twitch at the corners of his mouth.

"OK," he laughed. "OK. But help me get the old bat home!"

Great Aunt Izzy, however, had other ideas. She was having far too much fun to go home. She had organised all the kids into a very silly game of

"Grandmother's Footsteps" (in which everyone was the grandmother, except her), and she wasn't going to leave until she had won. And when Sam tried to take her arm, she giggled and disappeared up the climbing frame again.

Then things got worse. When they finally persuaded Aunt Izzy to leave the park, she stopped at the corner shop and refused to budge. The customers all stared at the strange old lady chanting *"Eeny, meeny, miney, mo"* at the oranges.

Emmy giggled nervously.

Suddenly Aunt Izzy picked up the oranges and began to juggle with them. Mr Grim came angrily out of his shop. It was that kid dressed up again.

"I'll teach you to juggle with my oranges," he shouted angrily.

"I wish you would," frowned Aunt Izzy as she dropped one. "I don't seem to be very good at it."

Mr Grim's face turned orange and beetroot (which nicely matched the display behind him). He grabbed hold of Aunt Izzy's shoulders, swung her round to face him – and his face now went pale. It *was* an old lady after all.

Leaving him stuttering and stammering, Aunt Izzy hitched up her skirt and leap-frogged over the banana boxes.

Sam had had enough. He grabbed Emmy and Aunt Izzy's hands and marched them both home. He was going to change Aunt Izzy back no matter what Emmy said. But what if he couldn't? He had a moment's panic. One Emmy was enough for anyone!

Chapter Six

However, hypnotising Great Aunt Izzy
back into her normal self proved to be
no problem after all. There were a
couple of worrying moments when Sam
thought the old lady wasn't going to
wake up at all, but on the third click of
his fingers Aunt Izzy sat up very
straight and announced it was time
for tea.

Sam sighed with relief. But Emmy felt sad that the afternoon was over. True, they hadn't managed to change Aunt Izzy at all, but it had been fun pretending to be an old lady and watching Aunt Izzy acting like her.

She giggled as she remembered Aunt Izzy swinging from the climbing frame, shouting orders to the other kids.

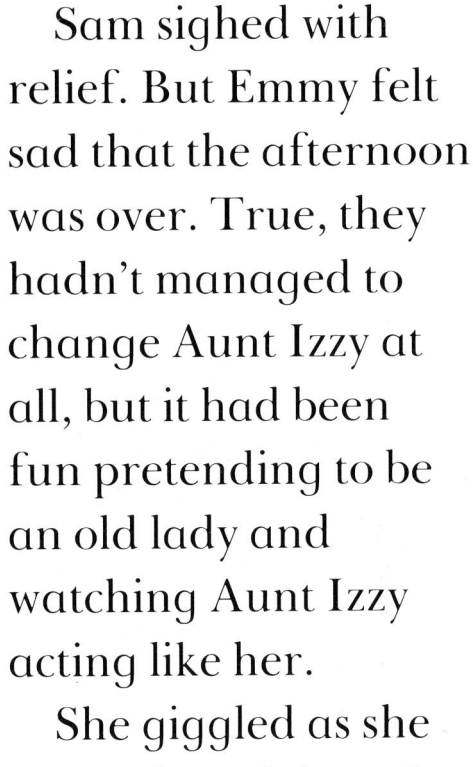

But did she really behave like that herself? Emmy frowned. She had to admit, Aunt Izzy had been a bit of a pain. . . .

She would have to try harder with the old battleaxe, Emmy decided uncomfortably. If she stopped telling so many jokes then perhaps she and Aunt Izzy would get on better.

Aunt Izzy silently put out the plates and cups.

"Does the knife go on my right hand or my left?" Emmy asked, knowing Aunt Izzy was keen on such things.

"Neither," said Aunt Izzy, with a twinkle in her eye. "It goes on the table, Emmeline."

Emmy looked astonished. That was just what she would have said! Maybe

Aunt Izzy hadn't been changed back properly. Emmy began to feel worried.

"Can I help you make the tea," asked Emmy. "Will the sandwiches be long?"

"No, sort of short and squarish," said Aunt Izzy, bringing in the sandwiches, and then laughing at Emmy and Sam's astonished faces.

"You know, I'm not as stuffy as I look," she said sitting down. "When I was a girl. . . ."

This time Emmy didn't interrupt, because the stories Aunt Izzy began to tell them were very different from those she had told before.

They were wonderful
stories, all about the
jokes Aunt Izzy and
her friends used to
play when they were
young, and the exciting games they had
had. Emmy and Sam listened in
astonishment. Was this the same Great
Aunt Izzy?

44

The more Emmy listened, the more she decided she liked Aunt Izzy. And the more Aunt Izzy talked, the more she seemed to enjoy herself.

"It's funny," said Aunt Izzy after a while. "I'd forgotten all those things until today. I wonder what made me remember?"

Emmy coughed and cleared the table.

Emmy was sad when the week was over. By the time her mum and dad got back, she and Aunt Izzy had become the best of friends. In fact, Emmeline Mary McGinty was now a dear funny girl who told wonderful jokes. At least her Great Aunt Izzy said so. And that same Great

Aunt Izzy was a brilliant storyteller and a pretty special Aunt. At least Emmeline Mary said so.

And so in the end the Great Aunt Izzy disaster wasn't such a disaster after all.